Schirmer's Library of Musical Classics

Vols. 1104-1105

ALBUM OF
SCANDINAVIAN PIANO MUSIC

FORTY-ONE PIECES

SELECTED, EDITED AND FINGERED BY
LOUIS OESTERLE
WITH BIOGRAPHICAL NOTES

IN TWO VOLUMES

1104. VOL. I, TWENTY-FIVE PIECES
1105. VOL. II, SIXTEEN PIECES

NEW YORK : G. SCHIRMER
BOSTON : THE BOSTON MUSIC CO.
COPYRIGHT, 1902, BY G. SCHIRMER

CONTENTS

VOL. I

		PAGE
ANDERSSON, R., Op. 14, No. 5	A la Gavotte	42
BÄCK, KNUT, Op. 7, No. 14	Like a Folk-song	21
BACKER-GRÖNDAHL, A., Op. 36, No. 3	Waltz	48
—— Op. 45, No. 3	Chant d' Été	14
BIRKEDAL-BARFOD, L., from Op. 7	Album-leaf	26
ENNA, A.	Barcarole	11
GRIEG, E., Op. 17, No. 5	Dance from Jölster	22
—— Op. 17, No. 18	Humoristic Dance	54
—— Op. 66, No. 15	Cradle-song	40
KJERULF, H.	Berceuse in D♭	24
LANGGAARD, S.	Love-song	59
LASSON, B.	Serenade	16
LASSON, PER	Crescendo	56
NEUPERT, E.	Fantasiestück No. 2	37
OLSEN, OLE	Berceuse	46
——	Fanitull	28
——	Legend	44
——	Mazurka	6
——	Serenade	32
——	Valse-Caprice	8
PHILIPPSON, M., Op. 13, No. 5	Pensée	18
SCHYTTE, L., Op. 12, No. 3	Le Soir	4
—— Op. 18, No. 1	Impromptu	34
—— Op. 35, No. 1	Scandinavian Dance	2
SINDING, C., Op. 24, No. 4	Characteristic Piece	51

VOL. II

AULIN, T., Op. 5, No. 2	Album-leaf	26
BÄCK, KNUT, Op. 7, No. 7	Novellette	2
BACKER-GRÖNDAHL, A., Op. 15, No. 1	Serenade	28
BECHGAARD, J.	Sonnet	39
ELLING, C., Op. 50, No. 2	Melody	37
ENNA, A., Op. 4, No. 1	Impromptu	48
—— Op. 4, No. 3	Humoreske	31
GRIEG, E., Op. 66, No. 18	"Thoughtfully I wander"	22
KJERULF, H.	Cradle-song in F♯	5
NORDRAAK, R.	Valse-Caprice	19
SCHYTTE, L., Op. 34, No. 7	Étude mélodique	13
SINDING, C., Op. 44, No. 5	Caprice	60
SJÖGREN, E.	Eroticon	42
WINDING, A., Op. 18, No. 1	Étude	52
—— Op. 34, No. 2	Notturno	56
WINGE, P.	Novellette	8

Scandinavian Dance.

LUDVIG SCHYTTE. Op. 35, No. 1.

Le Soir.
(Eventide.)

LUDVIG SCHYTTE. Op. 12, N° 3.

Mazurka.

OLE OLSEN.

Valse-Caprice.

OLE OLSEN.

Barcarole

Edited and fingered by
Louis Oesterle.

August Enna

Copyright, 1902, by G.Schirmer.

Summer-Song
Sommervise

Edited and fingered by Louis Oesterle

Agathe Backer-Gröndahl. Op.45, Nº 3

Serenade.

BREDO LASSON.
(1885)

I folkviseton.
(Like a Folk-song.)

KNUT BÄCK. Op. 7, N? 14.

Berceuse.
(Lullaby.)

Edited and fingered by *Louis Oesterle*.

H. KJERULF.

Album-leaf.

L. BIRKEDAL BARFOD, fr. Op. 7.

Fanitull.

The Fanitull, according to an old Norwegian legend, is a wild, mad dance once played by the devil, which became the heritage of the village musicians. When the tune of this dance resounded at peasant weddings, its effect was such, that desperate brawls ensued, in which it not seldom happened that some bold fighter lost his life.

OLE OLSEN.

Serenade

Edited and fingered by
Louis Oesterle

Ole Olsen

Impromptu.

LUDVIG SCHYTTE. Op. 18, No 1.

Tempo di minuetto.

Valse Caprice
Fantasiestück No.2

EDMUND NEUPERT

Bådnlåt.
(Cradle-song.)

EDVARD GRIEG. Op. 66, N°15.

À la Gavotte.

Allegro vivace. RICHARD ANDERSSON. Op.14, Nº 5.

Sagn.
(Legend.)

OLE OLSEN.

Vals.
(Waltz.)

AGATHE BACKER-GRÖNDAHL. Op. 36, N.º 3.

49

Stabbe-Laaten.
(Humoristic Dance.)

EDVARD GRIEG. Op. 17, N° 18.

Crescendo.

Revised and fingered by
Wm Scharfenberg.

PER LASSON.

Liebeslied.
(Love-song.)

LaVergne, TN USA
14 October 2009
160870LV00001B/172/P